When Charlie Feels Afraid

by
Brenda Sue Bynum

Illustrated by
Paul and Dee Gully

All Bible references in this book are from the King James Version except where noted.

Name: Bynum, Brenda Sue
Title: When Charlie Is Afraid by Brenda Sue Bynum
Illustrators. Paul and Deee Gully
Identifiers: LCCN: 2021919175
ISBN: 978-1-953114-16-7
Subjects: 1. JUV033090 JUVENILE FICTION/RELIGIOUS/CHRISTIAN/EMO-TIONS & FEELINGS
2. JUV033220 JUVENILE FICTION/SOCIAL ISSUES/BULLYING/STRANGERS
3. JUV043000 JUVENILE FICTION/SOCIAL THEMES/ SELF-ESTEEM & SELF-RELIANCEl

Published by EA Books Publishing, a division of
Living Parables of Central Florida, Inc. a 501c3

EABooksPublishing.com

ACKNOWLEDGEMENTS

Thanks to Peggy King Anderson for her passionate coaching to help others succeed. Thanks to Paul & Dee Gully for their creative artwork. Thanks to friends and family members who gave insight from personal experiences of keeping their children safe.

DEDICATION

This book is dedicated to all those serving vulnerable, exploited, and at-risk children, for showing them love and care. For all the children who feel afraid and alone, you are thought of every day by our heavenly Father. He desires that you come to Him.

"Come to Me, all you who labor and are heavy laden, and I will give you rest."
(Matthew 11:28. NKJV)

Being afraid is NOT
Charlie's favorite thing!
His stomach hurts,
and his hands get sweaty.

Many people feel afraid. Even King David, in the Bible, felt **AFRAID!**

When he was a young boy, he chased wild animals away from his sheep with his slingshot. But David felt afraid when another king wanted to harm him.

David had a good secret to help him when he felt afraid. His good secret was that he trusted God! David said, "In God have I put my trust: I will not be afraid what man can do unto me." *(Psalm 56:11)*

You can trust God, too!

Jonathan was David's good friend.
David talked to Jonathan about his fears.
YOU CAN talk to someone about things
that make you feel afraid, too. Sometimes
talking about it helps. YOU CAN learn
good things from others that might help
you feel better.

Like David, Charlie is learning helpful
things he can do when people, places,
and things make him feel afraid.
Maybe they can help you, too!

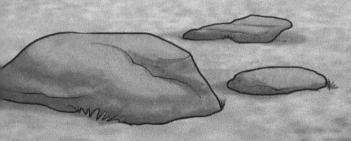

PEOPLE

Some **STRANGERS** make Charlie feel afraid.

When Charlie walks home after school, sometimes he sees STRANGERS. Some strangers smile at Charlie, some ignore him, and some want to talk to him. The strangers who want to talk to Charlie make him feel afraid, because he doesn't know them.

Not all strangers do bad things, but some might.

THINGS CHARLIE HAS LEARNED:

• He talks to his parents or teachers about the people who make him feel afraid.

• He asks a friend to walk with him after school and **NEVER** walks by himself.

• He yells, 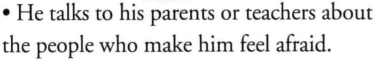 **"STOP! STRANGER! STRANGER!** if a stranger wants him to walk with them.

• He SCREAMS and runs away as fast as he can, if a stranger tries to get him to go with them. **"What would you do?"**

Some people are BULLIES.

Charlie is afraid of the school bully, Bud, and his friends. Bud calls Charlie names. It hurts to be bullied, and Charlie doesn't want to see other kids bullied, either. He likes to see kids smile and not be afraid!

THINGS CHARLIE HAS LEARNED:
- He tells the school bully,
"STOP! THOSE WORDS HURT!"

- He talks to his teacher or parents.
- He remembers what it feels like to be bullied. It hurts!"
Can you and your parents think of other helpful things
to do when you feel afraid of people?

PLACES

Places that make Charlie feel afraid
are places he should not go to alone.
On the way home from school,
he passes a sign that says, "Keep Out."
The old house on the other side of
the gate is falling apart. His fear keeps
him from this danger. Charlie can
listen to this fear because it helps
keep him from danger.

THINGS CHARLIE HAS LEARNED:
• He listens to his fear when he is
around dangerous places.
• He stays away from dangerous places.

Another place that makes Charlie feel afraid is a pond close to his home. Ducks and geese swim in the water. They quack and honk like his friend's bicycle horn. The pond smells like his sweaty socks. Charlie is afraid of the deep water because he can't swim.

THINGS CHARLIE HAS LEARNED:

- He stays away from the pond when he's by himself.
- He asks his parents to take him to the pond.

Do you have places you are afraid of? Can you and your parents think of ways for you to stay safe?

THINGS

Darkness makes Charlie feel afraid.
When he goes to bed at night and
the light goes out, his room is dark.
He can't see what's in the darkness.

What if a hairy-legged spider crawls on his arm or a stinky bear hides in the dark? Charlie feels afraid.

THINGS CHARLIE HAS LEARNED:
• Before bedtime, Charlie turns a small light on. Now it isn't totally dark in his room.
• He looks under his covers to see if there's a spider. No bear in the corner, either!
• He prays and asks God to keep him safe. He closes his eyes and sleeps.

What makes you feel afraid? What are some other things you and your parents can think of that would help you feel safe?

Scary pictures on TV
make Charlie feel afraid. When he
watches TV, he wants to hide when
people fight and hurt each other.
When people argue or say ugly words,
his stomach hurts. When movies, the
news, or commercials on TV show
people doing these things, Charlie gets
scared. Then, he has nightmares.

THINGS CHARLIE HAS LEARNED:

- When he watches TV, he closes his eyes
and covers his ears during scary pictures.
- He goes out of the room when scary
movies, the news, or commercials are on.
- He watches channels that do not have
scary programs.

**Can you and your parents think of other helpful
ideas you can do when you watch TV?**

Charlie's favorite things!

Charlie is NOT afraid to smile or draw pictures.
These are his favorite things! This is what Charlie
likes to do: He draws a circle on a piece of paper,
cuts it out, and draws a fear face on one side.

On the other side, he draws a smiley face. Charlie tells the fear face, "Go away, fear!" Then, he turns the fear face around to the smiley face and smiles! Charlie has learned some good things that help him when he feels afraid. He hopes you will, too!

Here's a prayer Charlie likes to pray:
"Dear God, give me courage when I feel afraid.
Help me to be strong and brave,
the way you helped David. Amen."

Here's a song from more of David's words
that Charlie likes to sing. It sounds like
The Farmer in the Dell, or you can make
your own tune or a rap.
David called on God's name.
YOU CAN do the same!

What time I am afraid,
What time I am afraid,
What time I am afraid,
I will put my trust in God!
What time I am afraid,
I will trust in thee.

What time I am afraid,
I will trust in thee. Psalm 56:3

Thank you for reading *When Charlie Feels Afraid.*
Like Charlie, I like to draw faces, and sometimes I feel afraid, too.
The activities I have written in this book help me when I feel afraid.
I hope you will find them helpful, too. I want you to be happy and
not afraid. But when you do feel afraid,
I want you to know that it's OK to talk
about your fears and ask for help.

Remember, God wants to help you
when you feel afraid. I am going to
draw you a happy face because I am
glad you read my book.

Additional children's books by the Author and Illustrators are available on Amazon:

Paul and Dee Gully are a husband and wife team working together to illustrate children's books. They love helping authors bring their books to life. Their hope is that the illustrations will allow readers to experience the love and grace of Jesus Christ! Below are a few books to help children through tough and scary times in their lives. See more of their books and illustrations at:

www.pancakeparables.com

CPSIA information can be obtained
at www.ICGtesting.com
Printed in the USA
BVHW062026281021
619992BV00002B/39